P9-AQG-062

2014

Planting a Rainbow

Written and illustrated by Lois Ehlert

Harcourt, Inc.

ORLANDO   AUSTIN   NEW YORK   SAN DIEGO   LONDON

DEDICATED TO SHIRLEY AND DICK

For information about permission to reproduce selections from this book, please write Permissions, Houghton Mifflin Harcourt Publishing Company 215 Park Avenue South NY NY 10003.

www.hmhbooks.com

Library of Congress Cataloging-in-Publication Data
Ehlert, Lois.
Planting a rainbow.
Summary: A mother and child plant a rainbow of flowers in the family garden.
[1. Gardening—Fiction. 2. Flowers—Fiction.
3. Mother and child—Fiction.] I. Title.
PZ7.E3225P1 1988 [E]—dc19 87-8528
ISBN 978-0-15-262609-9
ISBN 978-0-15-262610-5 pb
ISBN 978-0-15-262611-2 oversize pb

Printed and bound by Tien Wah Press, Malaysia

TWP 38 37 36
4500396349

Printed in Malaysia

Every year Mom and
I plant a rainbow

In the fall we buy some bulbs

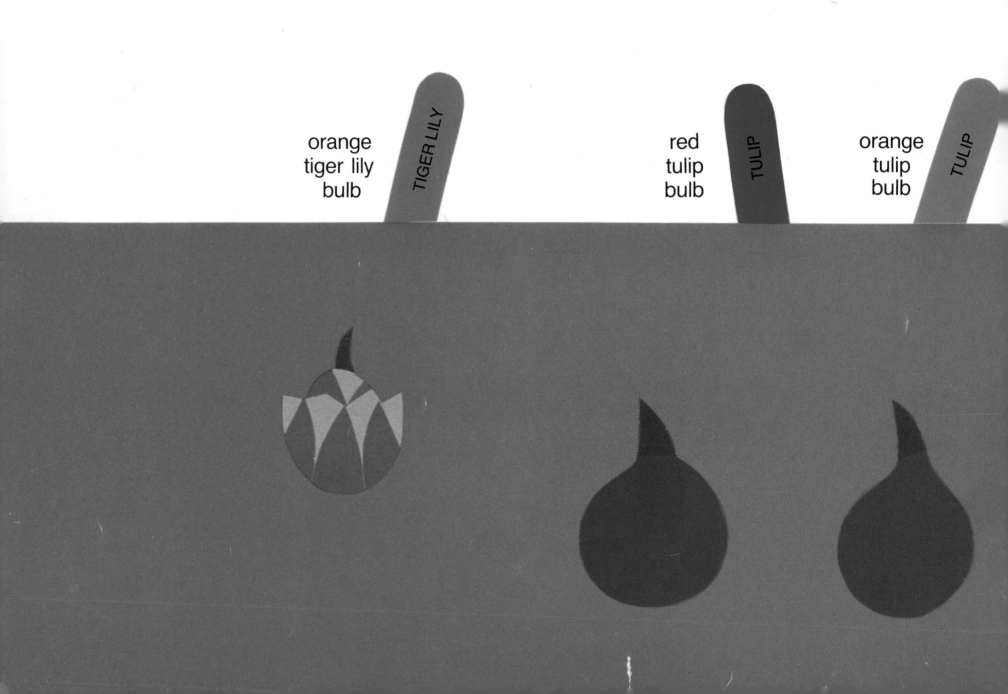

orange
tiger lily
bulb

TIGER LILY

red
tulip
bulb

TULIP

orange
tulip
bulb

TULIP

and plant them in the ground.

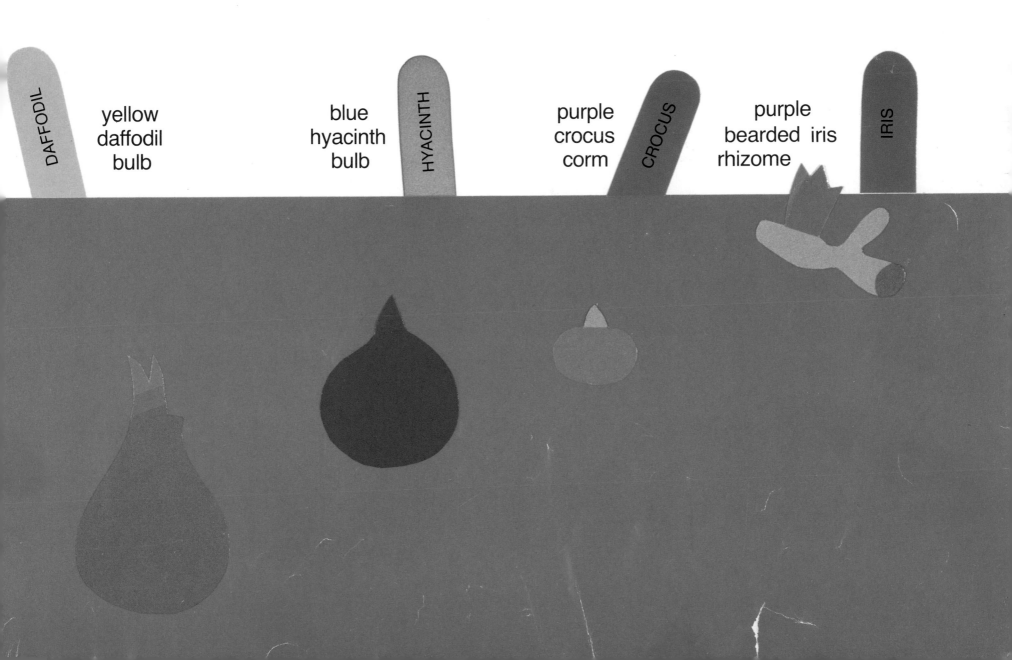

DAFFODIL

yellow
daffodil
bulb

blue
hyacinth
bulb

HYACINTH

purple
crocus
corm

CROCUS

purple
bearded iris
rhizome

IRIS

We order seeds from catalogs and

Phlox

Morning Glory

Zinnia

wait all winter long

Aster

Cornflower

Marigold

Daisy

for spring to warm the soil
and sprout the bulbs.

TULIP

TULIP

DAFFODIL

HYACINTH

CROCUS

Then it's time to go to the garden center to select some seedlings.

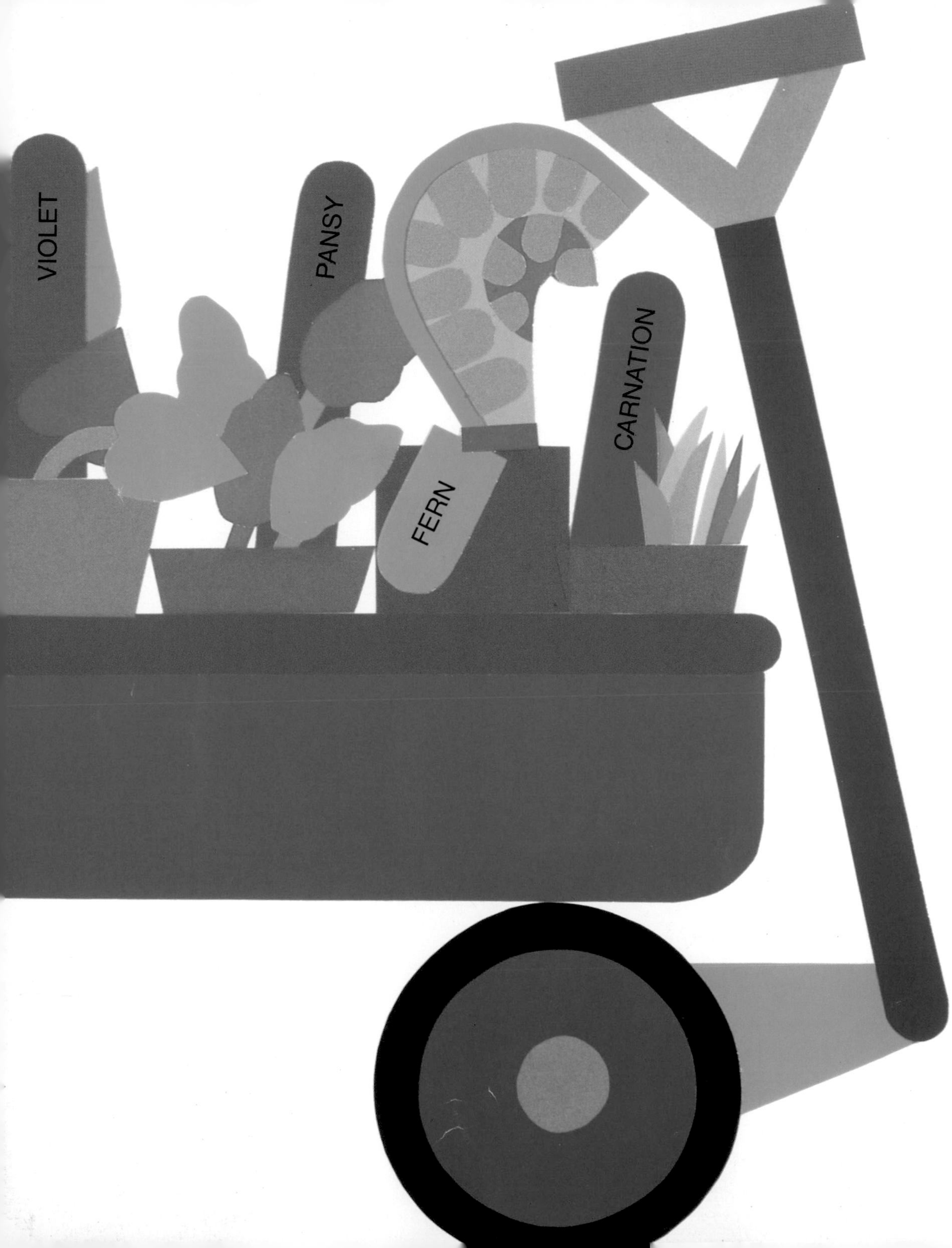
VIOLET
PANSY
CARNATION
FERN

We sow the seeds and set out the

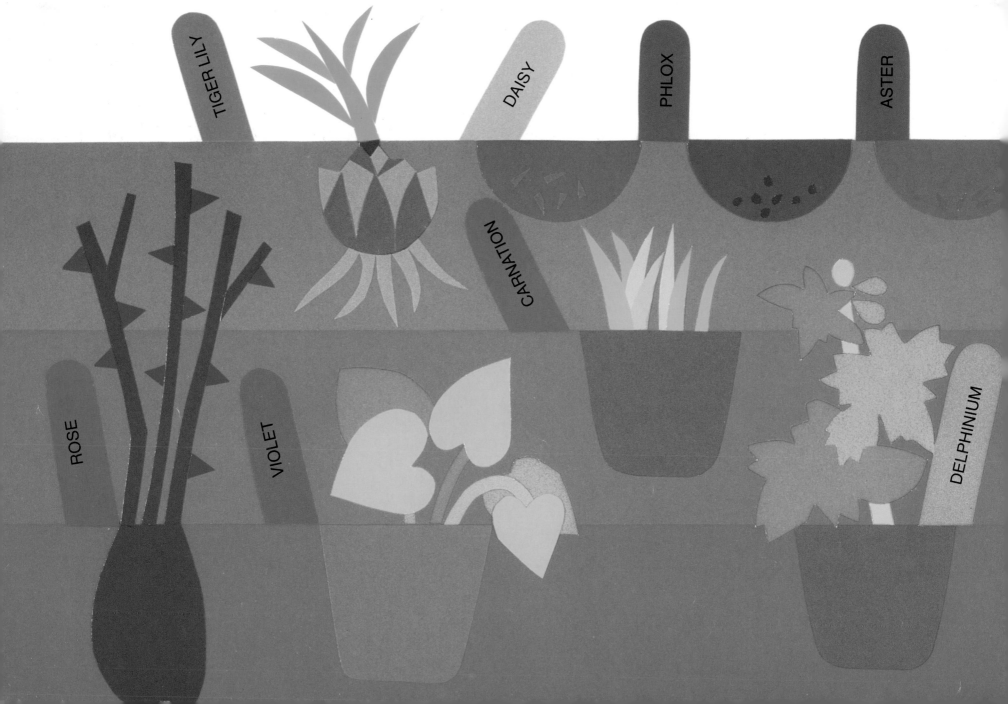

plants in soil,

MARIGOLD

ZINNIA

MORNING GLORY

CORNFLOWER

IRIS

PANSY

POPPY

FERN

and watch the

rainbow grow,

MARIGOLD

ZINNIA

MORNING GLORY

CORNFLOWER

IRIS

PANSY

POPPY

FERN

and grow,

and grow.

carnations

tulips

We have some red flowers

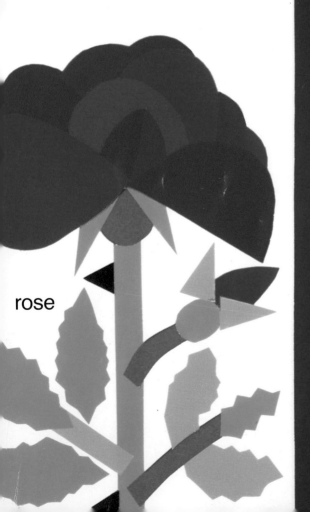

rose

zinnia

and
orange
flowers,

tulip

poppy

tiger lily

and
some blue
flowers,

We
so
gro

morning
glories

delphinium

hyacinth

cornflowers

and some
purple
flowers,
too.

phlox

crocus

iris

violets

asters

pansy

All summer long
we pick them
and bring them home.

And when summer is over, we know we can grow our rainbow again next year.